STEVENSON UNDER
THE PALM TREES

STEVENSON UNDER THE PALM TREES

Alberto Manguel

CANONGATE U.S.
New York

First published in Great Britain in 2004 by
Canongate Books Ltd., Edinburgh, Scotland

Printed in the United States of America

FIRST AMERICAN EDITION

ISBN 1-84195-588-4

Canongate U.S.
841 Broadway
New York, NY 10003

04 05 06 07 08   10 9 8 7 6 5 4 3 2 1

*No one wanders under
palm trees unpunished.*
Goethe,
Elective Affinities

To Craig, the other Stevenson, with all my love.

Robert Louis Stevenson left the house and walked the long trek down to the beach just as the day was setting. From the verandah the sea was hidden by the trees, six hundred feet below, filling the end of two vales of forest. To enjoy the last plunge of the sun before the clear darkness set in, the best observation-post was among the mangrove roots, in spite (he said bravely to himself) of the mosquitoes and the sand-flies. He did not immediately notice the figure because it appeared to be merely one more crouching shadow among the shadows, but then it turned and seemed for a moment to be watching him. The man was wearing a broad-rimmed hat not unlike Stevenson's own and,

1

even though he could see that the skin was white, he could not make out the man's features.

'It goes down so quickly, you would think the water put out the flames,' Stevenson said to break the silence.

'And so it does,' the man answered, without standing up, and Stevenson joyfully recognised in the voice a robust Scots accent which, to his sorrow, was dying out in the better parts of Edinburgh.

'I don't think we've met,' he smiled, coming up to the stranger with a welcoming hand. The white population of Apia was not large and Stevenson, Samoa's chief celebrity, had been introduced, alas, to all.

'Baker,' the man said. 'And of course, I know who you are. I've been island-hopping for only the Lord knows how long, and even as far as Tonga your name is mentioned. I sometimes claim blood-ties with you to foster my own cause.'

'And that may be?'

'The Cause of the True Way, the cause of all good men. Officially, I draw up a sort of census of missionary work in this god-forsaken ocean. We like to keep an eye on these things. The Edinburgh Missionary Society.'

Stevenson sat down on a root and looked up into the sky. The stars were out and the sea was white.

'When did you leave Edinburgh?' he asked.

'Longer ago than I care to remember,' the man said. 'Now the city lies so far away, it hardly exists.'

'For me, the contrary is true,' Stevenson said. 'The distance has made it even more present than when I lived there. I go to sleep with its cold dampness in my nostrils and I wake up with the smoke of its chimneys in my eyes.'

'A good climate to steel the soul, I say. Here the heat softens the sinews, makes sin burst like flowers from the mud.' He scooped up a handful of wet sand and let it trickle through his fingers.

'And how long do you intend to stay in Samoa?' Stevenson asked less out of curiosity than out of a desire to hear the man's voice again.

'Until my work is done,' the man answered.

Later that evening, as supper was being prepared in the big hall of the House at Vailima, Stevenson mentioned the encounter to his wife who observed that there were far too many Scotsmen let loose in the world. 'This one's of the cold breed,' Stevenson remarked, almost to himself, and then wondered what exactly his ancestors had meant by that phrase.

The next day there was to be a feast up in the village and even before sunrise the carts could be heard carrying in supplies: the voices of the men, singing, the women calling after the children, the squeals of the pigs about to be slaughtered, the hacking of wood, the thundering fall of a coconut tree. Standing on the verandah, watching the vegetation soak up the growing light, Stevenson thought of how different the activities of life were here, under the hot sky, than in the place he used to call home and that he still, at times, longed for. He sometimes felt that he needed, in a physical sense, the edge of frosty cold and black rain, and the dour look of the Edinburgh stones, grey with a tinge of pink, like the rotting corpse of a mouse. Here things decayed in splendour, obscenely. He remembered his first year in Samoa and the yard covered in fallen papayas – the bright yellow skin turning dark, the fruit opening its many folds and exposing its sensuous, fleshy inside, smelling of saliva – and how he and Fanny had turned away without saying a word, as if they had unwittingly come upon a private and lewd spectacle. There had been

7

a woman once, in a brothel near Perpignan, who had sat on a bench by the door as he came in, her legs impossibly open, and he had been both repulsed and dazzled by her sight, at a nakedness deeper than any nakedness he had ever known. In Samoa, the nakedness of women, which so troubled the missionaries, was never ugly. In the evening, when the villagers would go down to the sea to bathe, splashing in the waves with the children, the women's thick black tangled hair opened like anemones in the water, while the hibiscus which they wore behind the ears would drift away around them, like fiery islands. Standing on the pier, Stevenson loved watching them, their dark skin as brilliant and hard as volcanic stones.

Here in Samoa, everything that had been reserved, whispered, buttoned-up in the cloistered world of his childhood, was out in the open – brash, unhidden – and in the beginning it had overwhelmed his senses and choked him, as it had upset Fanny and made her impatient and angry. But they had stayed on, and over the years the loudness of it all had charmed them, and they had grown accustomed to the lack of reserve. And even if they maintained at home, at Vailima, the proprieties due to a Scottish gentleman and his American wife and their family (his two grown step-children, his aged mother), they now rejoiced in the riot of colours and sounds outside, and in the sight of a world that seems to be constantly opening up, like a heavily-scented flower.

After breakfast, Fanny sat in the large hall going over the accounts, and he tried to read the London papers: he had been sick during the night, as usual, and now he felt that his head was not willing to do any work. He read, as if recalling a vague memory, names that were familiar to him but that he could not quite place, and he thought, as he did so often these days, how curious it was that the place he had once known so well had been taken over so utterly by such an unexpected geography, the remembered sensations of one mingling with the encroaching sensations of the other. He read of gossip and goings-on in the faraway island of Britain with the interest of a keen anthropologist, and it amused him to imagine his friends doing the same, as they pictured 'old RLS among the savages of Samoa'.

Around eleven, Sosimo, the overseer, came in to say that the cart was ready. The whole family climbed in – Stevenson, Fanny, old Mrs Thomas Stevenson and Fanny's children, Belle Strong and Lloyd Osbourne – and Sosimo whipped the mule into a trot.

The village had been decorated with branches of palm and strings of flowers. In front of newly stretched-out sheets of tapa, the drummers, crowned with triple wreaths of tiare flowers, were rehearsing with more good humour than skill, and a few of the younger girls, all giggles, were swinging their hips to the

10

rhythm. Two or three of the elders came out to meet the Stevenson clan, and helped the ladies down from the cart. Mrs Thomas Stevenson, clutching her black parasol, jumped to the ground with surprising agility and was led off by a group of older women who started at once a cackling stream of gossip. Lloyd Osbourne offered to help carry the mats Sosimo was unloading from the cart, while Stevenson, protected by his wide-brimmed hat, and Fanny and Belle, shaded by their small white parasols, were conducted to the circle near the dug-out ovens. For a while, they watched the meat and the bundles of food being lowered onto the hot stones, all in the midst of great clouds of smoke. Then the ovens were covered with green palm leaves and the chief invited them to sit. Chairs were brought out for Fanny and Belle, but Stevenson sat crossed-legged with the other men.

People were coming and going, children

11

were running, thin dogs sniffed in every corner until someone kicked them away, an odd chicken crossed the main circle at a flustered clip. Stevenson had never quite enjoyed what his childhood nurse, in her thick north-country brogue, had called 'popular intemperance': the movements of a crowd, unpredictable and strong as a blaze. In the midst of a large group of people, joyful or angry, mourning or seeking merriment, he felt naked, and he had tried, often, to overcome that feeling, which for want of a keener word he called shyness, but which his father had once branded cowardice, an accusation he had not forgotten. Now, something like a crowd began to assemble around them, and Stevenson forced himself to feel at ease, or look as if he felt at ease. Then the music began in earnest.

When they first arrived in Samoa, Stevenson had wondered whether the strange customs of the alien place would offend his mother. He had read about them and longed to see what they were in the flesh, and he suspected that Fanny, in spite of her American puritanism, as a faithful reader of Walt Whitman, would no doubt be capable of enjoying a healthy display of the human figure, clothed not by the wind and rain, but by the sun. What concerned him was how his mother would react to the bare black flesh and the swaying movements, the teeth that were too white and the hair too black for the simple Edinburgh lady, accustomed to bodies clad in stiff dark silks edged with lace. First in Hawaii and then in Tahiti, where the human face had slender features and the hair was long and straight, and later in these islands where the features became rounder, the skin far darker and the hair curled in thickly matted crowns, Mrs Thomas Stevenson had seemed merely to rejoice in the variety on God's earth and delight in the multiplicity of His own image. She compared the Tahitian faces to golden lilies and the Samoan faces to inky roses, and everywhere she felt welcome. Stevenson watched her now, happily seated among the Samoan matrons, her slate-coloured dress and white face, hair and hands the shadow reflection of their white mumus and black skin.

The drums beat out a persistent rhythm that grew subtly, steadily, and a row of men, dabs of paint on their cheeks and green wreaths around their heads, began dancing in a straight line, while the women sang in counterpoint an encouraging chorus. Then it was the women's turn, and they lifted their arms and swayed with wave-like motions, side to side, in perfect unison. Now the adolescents joined in, some more awkwardly or shyly than others, and suddenly Stevenson saw one girl of extraordinary beauty, moving with full confidence to the music.

She must have been thirteen or fourteen, her thick hair held away from her forehead by a string of tiare flowers, the black waves falling over her thin shoulders, a large red hibiscus bloom open behind her ear. Her small breasts were visible under a strip of coloured cloth (a concession to the visiting missionary), and as she swayed, her straw skirt decorated with shells and beads revealed her long slender legs. Stevenson loved her eyes, and as he watched her, she caught his look and smiled. Embarrassed, and surprised at being embarrassed, Stevenson turned his head. When he looked again, she had disappeared behind the drummers with several of the other girls. The beat changed. A large man began to dance alone in the centre of the circle.

All the rest of the day, Stevenson caught and lost sight of the girl when he least expected it. He looked out for her during the long speech by the chief, and afterwards, as they sat drinking the kava and eating the pork and taro root, but he didn't see her. Then she suddenly appeared bearing a dish of baked breadfruit, and later, among the

15

older women, combing someone's hair, and then, for a moment, laughing with a couple of friends in the shade of a flame-tree. Once, he turned around and saw her watching him, but as he turned she ran away.

Many years before, in France, he had seen a girl of much the same age bathing behind a tattered screen in the courtyard of a farm, and he had felt this now-remembered surge of desire. Saint Augustine, he thought it was, had thanked God for not making him responsible for his dreams. He took a long drink of kava and uttered the same prayer of thanks.

The coughing began as it so often did, without warning, first as a rasping in the back of his throat and then a hacking, dry splutter that seemed never to end. His whole frame shook and pain shot up through his temples and down under his ribcage. Fanny put her arm around him, but he shook her off and tried to stand up, conscious that the villagers were watching him. Lloyd Osbourne came over and led him away, to the waiting cart, but before they had reached it, the cough became so violent that he began to tremble. For a long moment, he felt that his knees were giving way and, just before losing consciousness, he saw in the handkerchief he held before his mouth a large bright stain, as crimson as the flower the girl wore in her hair.

In the morning, he woke feeling curiously better than he had in a long time, as if the wracking cough had passed like a storm, leaving him almost refreshed, without even his usual shortness of breath. Fanny wanted him to stay in bed but he wouldn't hear of it. He felt full of delicious energy, and, after breakfast, he sat down to write a new chapter of the dark Scottish romance he was composing. There was an urgency in his every gesture that puzzled and delighted him. He was anxious to get started. He sat down, straightened the brief row of books on his desk, pulled several sheets of paper from under the blotter and dipped his pen in the ink.

Though Lloyd or Belle usually took down his dictation because of the scrivener's cramp that now added itself to his old list of afflictions, he preferred, whenever possible, to hold the pen himself and see the story literally flow onto the page. Today, as if by miracle, the writing went beautifully well: in the strong southern sunlight, he conjured up with ease the wind and the rain of Scotland, and the rich, careful language of his forebears. He had once remarked to Henry James that what he wished to do was to starve the visual sense in his books. He heard people talking, he felt them acting, and that was for him the definition of fiction. He made a note of his two literary aims:

1st. War on the *adjective*
2nd. Death to the *optic nerve*

Now he saw his villain cross the stormy heath in a passion and heard him justify himself to the Lord God of Hosts in sentences that rolled and rumbled like thunder. The girl at the feast lent her smile to the character of the young woman in his romance, and Stevenson told himself that this was possession enough: 'a permissible sin' he said to himself, and he was grateful for it.

The story of right and wrong held his attention as it unravelled itself in his mind's eye, and he felt contented in its very simplicity. He wrote until midday and then stopped. It was too hot to walk down to the beach again, so he wandered out into the garden to stretch his tightened muscles.

Sosimo was gathering the fallen breadfruit and Stevenson asked him whether he had seen the new missionary that morning.

'No new missionary in Vailima,' Sosimo answered. 'Too many of them already in Apia.'

* * *

19

He thought no more about the girl. Instead, for the next few days, Stevenson looked out for his mysterious fellow countryman, moved by nostalgia for the Edinburgh drawl and a childlike need for knowing that everything was in its place. As he dictated the next chapters to Belle, he heard the missionary's tones mark the rhythm of his sentences. He asked Sosima twice again and received the same reply and, in the evenings, went down to the beach where he had first met Mr Baker. He wondered with whom he might be lodging, and how it was possible for him to have avoided the overseer's all-observant eyes and alert ears. A week later, when Stevenson had concluded that the missionary must have moved on to another island, the two men met once again in the same spot on the beach.

'This poisonous brightness,' Mr Baker said, shielding his eyes from the sun. 'The burning brightness of hell.'

Stevenson laughed and asked him where he

was staying. Mr Baker didn't answer directly.

'I've been busy on the other side of Apia. A census like this isn't easy to compile.'

'Do you simply write down the names?'

'Oh, no. Names are the least of it. Activities are what interest me. What work the devil finds for idle hands. I look in vain for doers of the word, not hearers only. And this place breeds sloth.'

'But you are comfortable with your board?'

'Comfortable enough. I never see my host and he never sees me, and therefore we get on splendidly. He is not a cultured man but he has some of your books in his house.'

'I sometimes think my publisher gives away copies to make me feel important.'

'I've never read them and never will. I have no time for the claptrap of fiction. Invented stories, indeed! Lies, I say, if you'll forgive me. Our short time on this earth is meant to be one of redress, of learning, not of dissipation and fantasies. There is only one Book, Sir, to which I owe all my attention, and it does not tell fables.'

Stevenson felt he was being accused. 'All I mean to do with my tales is to lend a little excitement, a little happiness. That is our obligation too, is it not?'

'Happiness?' The man chuckled. 'Happiness is a reward, not a right. Have you seen what filth the natives get up to here on the beach, late at night, in this so-called paradise?' His voice grew harsh. 'I have even seen white men, Europeans . . .' He broke off. 'No, Sir. I don't believe in the obligation of happiness.'

He woke up with a fierce hot pain in the joints of his right hand, and yet the idea that had come to him during the night would not bear dictating. He thanked his stepdaughter but told her he would do some work on his own that morning and sat down at his desk. He felt feverish and his fingers shook slightly, but he dutifully dipped his pen in the ink and began to write. He knew that the story had broken off, taken an unexpected sideroad. Darker and more violent the story came, and seemed to unearth vile, unspeakable things in its wake. He stopped for a moment, partly because of the pain and partly because of the horror that the story produced in him, but then he carried on, driven by a stronger need. On and on he wrote, his handwriting barely legible now because of the shaking. He covered twenty pages without a single erasure. He stopped when he heard his wife's voice outside the door. His face was drenched in sweat.

He told Fanny he would not be taking lunch and that he would go lie down and see whether the pain would pass. Then he told her he had written something quite different, and would she care to take a look at it. It had become a habit: she always read everything he wrote and a story stood or fell on her approval. His flushed face and laboured breathing worried her, but he brushed off her attempt to help him to the bedroom. She knew he hated being fussed over, and she let him go.

Sleep came but was far from restful. No breeze drifted through the bamboo shutters and even the streaked light felt hot and full of dust, stinging his shut eyes, so that he dreamed of being buried alive in an immense furnace. He awoke to the deafening sound of crickets, and found himself tangled in the wet sheet. As in the very beginning, he once more longed for Edinburgh. As he poured water into the wash-basin, he saw his face in the mirror and it looked red as if burnt by the sun.

He went downstairs. Fanny was sitting in the leather armchair, the manuscript on her lap.

'And?' he asked.

She took a moment to answer. Then she spoke:

'This is dreadful. It is crass. It is unseemly. The story you were writing was dark but powerful, on its way to being a masterpiece. This is . . . worse than sensationalism. And totally unsuitable for fiction.'

'Unsuitable for fiction?'

'I would have wished you hadn't allowed yourself even to dream such things. This is poison.'

He was furious. He felt his cheeks flush with rage and, without saying another word, snatched the pages from her hands. He stormed out of the room. Never had he felt so impassioned, so outraged. He looked at what he had written that morning and the words seemed to acquire a life of their own, snaking across the page in a handwriting he didn't recognize.

He read for a few moments, as if in a daze. Then he went up to the hearth, threw the manuscript on the stones and lit a match. He watched the paper crackle, grow red and then darken. When there was nothing left but smouldering ashes, he drew himself back downstairs. Fanny had not moved. He drew himself up to her, kneeled down by her side and put his head on her lap.

'You are right. I have absolutely missed the heart of the story. I have been misled, I don't know how. Will you forgive me?'

She combed her fingers through his hair. Neither he nor Fanny ever mentioned those pages again.

'I've written moral fables,' said Stevenson to Mr Baker, the next time they met.

A group of naval officers had come to pay their respects at Vailima, and the master of the house had fled to seek a little private peace before supper, leaving Fanny and his step-children to entertain the guests. He had found Mr Baker once again near the mangrove trees, apparently watching a couple of battling crabs fight their way across the sand.

'I think you can learn through stories

almost better than through sermons. Stories give you more to think about, because they are less to the point.'

'Exactly: less to the point is the wide, winding road. And I surely don't need to remind a connoisseur of John Knox to where such a road will lead. There is only one tale that need be told, and that tale requires no re-writings.'

The moon hid behind a few clouds and all that was left in the darkness was the deep Edinburgh voice. When it emerged again, only one of the silver crabs scuttled across the sand towards the incoming tide.

'Do you know Salamander Island, off the coast of New Guinea?' the voice continued. 'I was there three, maybe four years ago. It doesn't matter. The natives are as savage as you may care, or not care, to meet, and speak a tongue marvelously different from any other spoken on earth. A missionary settled there a few years before my arrival, intent on bringing the word of God to these bestial people. It took him many months to learn their language, and once he had mastered it, he proceeded to translate into their grunts and squeals Saint Paul's Letter to the Ephesians, in which, as you remember, the Apostle entreats the heathen to follow the Lord, not with eyeservice, as menpleasers, but as servants of Christ. Several years this man spent translating the holy words into the tongue of the Salamander people, labouring day and night. But the ways of the flesh, as I need not remind you, are weak, and those who have not felt the piercing of the nails and thorns are defenceless against the evils of this world. One by one the natives fell victims to a simple disease, a mild form of smallpox that the man of God had contracted before his journey, and when I arrived on the island there were barely a handful of weak and emaciated men and women left to greet me. A few weeks later, when the missionary had completed his useful endeavour and the last word of Saint Paul's letter had been penned in that primitive tongue, the sole remaining Salamander native took to his hut, never to emerge again. He was buried with his fellows who had gone before him to what they blindly called the sea beyond the sea. My brave missionary had completed his work, the translation of the Apostle's word in a tongue that now no one spoke, except himself. You say this matters? Not at all: it only proves that the Word will always outlast the flesh.'

'But we need stories, don't we, to teach us through the example?'

'Example of what? Your father was an engineer, I believe. What use were to him the exploits of Ivanhoe or the nonsense of Don Quixote? Facts and figures were what he built on, and so must I. To raise tall lights to guide us, far from the rocks of deceit.'

'The natives like stories. They are their

history, you see. They listen to mine, sometimes. They call me "Tusitala", the teller of
tales.'

Then he added:

'In this part of the world, the stories you
tell become part of reality. Do you know what
I mean? I wrote a story once about a magic
wishing-bottle. Well, after I read it one night
to a group from the village, they asked to see
the bottle. They still do, from time to time.
They think I have it. They think it's real,
because it appeared in a story. Anything else
would be a lie in their eyes.'

'Superstition, that is all it is. You would
be better employed reading to them from the
Scriptures. That is the only truth. And now,
if you'll excuse me.'

Stevenson watched him stand up and dis-
appear among the mangroves which, in the
rising waters, looked like many-footed animals
coming down to drink.

*   *   *

30

He heard the sound of voices outside and then Sosimo's voice calling him. He told Fanny he'd go find out what was happening, put on his housecoat and went downstairs. A group of native men were arguing in the front hall and Sosimo seemed to be trying to keep them calm. Through the open door, he could see a number of large women dressed in the white of mourning, wailing softly.

'Master,' Sosimo said. 'These men want to see you. Something bad has happened. Vaera, Tootei's daughter,' he pointed at a large man with an enormous stomach, 'was killed last night.'

Stevenson suddenly recognized the man as one of the drummers at the feast. He looked different now, without the crown of flowers and with a large white shirt buttoned up over his belly.

'How? Where? Has the chief justice been informed?'

'He has, and he is asking questions in

the village. But Tootei wishes to talk to you.'

'Come,' Tootei said. 'Come with us.'

'Come where?'

'He thinks you can help, Master. He thinks that by seeing the place you might know.'

Stevenson hesitated. Then he answered. 'I will come. Give me a minute.'

He went upstairs and told Fanny what had happened. Then he dressed, had a quick cup of black coffee and joined the men at the door.

The path led through a grove of papaya trees out into the fields and up the mountainside beyond. It was a difficult climb, because of the insects and the heat, but he enjoyed the strain on his muscles. Sweat was running down his scalp and he rubbed his handkerchief over his hair to dry it. Someone had told him admiringly that he worked harder than a man with twice his health, and he knew it was true.

During the long nights of his childhood, when, gasping for breath and shaken by a hollow cough, he had sat up in his bed, with his nurse by his side, waiting for what they called the Night Hag to finish her ghastly business and go, he had told himself that if ever he had enough strength, he would use it to lead his body to the edge of any possible adventure; he would take to the road or the sea, he would set off like a new Ulysses in the hope of strange encounters but, above all, he would travel for the sake of the journey itself. He had imagined his sick bed as a boat into which his nurse would help him every night and then, when the lights went out, he would cast off into the blue darkness, breathing lightly. In this hope he had waited for morning.

Now, above the tree-line, he could make out the hot sea below and the thin strip of grey beach. Further they climbed, and here the air was thinner and cooler. At last they reached the remains of a hut, close to the large bald stones where now-faded petroglyphs could once be seen.

The girl's body had been taken away but the crushed grass and the stained earth told the story.

'Can you see something, Tusitala?' Tootei asked. 'Is there anything to tell?'

Stevenson looked at the expectant man and shook his head.

'I can't tell anything, Tootei. I can't tell what happened. Be confident, however. I am certain the chief justice will help.'

Tootei sat down on his haunches.

'And I am certain he won't. The chief justice knows no stories.'

They remained on the hilltop for a long while, Tootei and the other men waiting for Stevenson to begin. Finally Sosimo got up and started the slow climb back down. The others followed.

*   *   *

All that afternoon and the next day, Stevenson felt as if his lungs would burst. First he sat on the verandah, hoping that sheer stillness would bring him relief; then he asked Fanny to help him with the American inhaler. She poured the powders into boiling water and then set the contraption above it and attempted a joke, as they always did, about Haroun al-Rachid and his magical hookah. But this time, the powders seemed to exacerbate the cough and soon there were red stains again on the handkerchief he held to his mouth. Fanny lifted him from under the arms and helped him to bed. Once more, he remarked to himself how strong she was, like a man, and, not unkindly, how her age had begun to show in the deep lines on her face. The face of the girl at the feast superimposed itself on Fanny's, and then on the dead body of Tootei's daughter, and he closed his eyes hard against the vision.

Propped against the pillows, the crumpled handkerchief in his hand and the basin at his reach, he let himself fall into a feverish sleep in which the scorching mountainside, female shapes, the swaying flame-trees and the drops of blood mingled in his dream as if in a demented geography.

When he woke, night had fallen. Fanny was sitting by the side of his bed, reading under the light of the tall petrol lamp they had bought in Hawaii. He looked at her concentrated face, the serious mouth he knew so well, the rough, hard-worked hands, and thought how everything in this place was now hideously familiar: the chair in which she sat came from his parents' house in Edinburgh; the engraving of the Raeburn portrait was a gift from Andrew Lang; the bed covers had been stitched by a friend of his mother's; the cabinet that had reputedly belonged to a notorious Edinburgh criminal and around which his nurse had woven many an uncanny yarn. Even the book his wife was reading, Barbey d'Aurévilly's *Les Diaboliques*, had been sent to him by the editor of *Scribners' Magazine*, two long years before.

The death of the child on the mountain was atrocious, did not bear thinking about. Guiltily he asked himself: where was the healthy novelty, where the good excitement that had filled his days earlier on? When would he find again in dirt and sweat the thrill he now found only in his own imagination, in the stories he told himself and which he tried, sometimes, to tell on the page? The real stuff was now shreds of memories: that distant afternoon, in the Cevennes mountains, when he had come across the two demonic strangers at Notre-Dame des Neiges; or that other time, when he had conversed for many hours with the large, lunatic woman in Father Damian's leper colony near Honolulu; or that night in San Francisco, when (he could not remember the Chinaman's name) had taken him to a place near the docks where his fortune had been told by reading the lees of tea at the bottom of a bowl. The word 'nostalgia' (he remembered having read somewhere) had been invented in the seventeenth century by an Alsatian student in a medical thesis, to describe the malady that afflicted Swiss soldiers when far from their native mountains. For him it was the contrary: nostalgia was the pain of missing places that he had never seen before.

He had suddenly grown old; maybe that's what it was. He had turned forty-four and that was no longer an age to go exploring.

Someone had once observed that the romantic life did not suit the writer of romances: that a man did not write better adventure stories by learning to chop wood and skin a hare. Perhaps now that life had become commonplace, that routine had set in and that the same things returned his indifferent glance day in, day out, now that there was no ardour left in his nights with Fanny who, out of concern for his health or out of mere lassitude, barely brushed a goodnight kiss on his cheek before falling asleep, perhaps now he might write something worthwhile, full of true blood and real thunder. With the exception of that dark excursus that had so offended Fanny, the present book was advancing nicely and he felt that he was being ungrateful to the fates who had allowed him this moment of grace.

This time the bout lasted several weeks. Every time he thought he felt stronger and tried to raise himself out of bed, he would fall back in a paroxism of coughing that would again stain the handkerchief and leave a murderous swirl in the bowl. Dr Funk, the family doctor with an impossible name, came and went several times but, as he told Fanny, there was nothing much to do except wait and pray, and trust that the body would recover on its own.

About a month later, when Stevenson was feeling well enough to sit up and even spend a few hours in his study, not actually writing but going through the abandoned manuscript with a critical pen, Sosimo came to tell him that Tootei was there again and wanted to see him.

Stevenson rose slowly and went to the door, stretching out his hand with a greeting. Tootei refused to take it.

'Have I offended you in some way?' Stevenson asked, surprised.

'You remember my daughter?'

'I never met her, Tootei, but I remember what a terrible thing happened to her. I also heard that they never found the murderer.'

'You did see her, Tusitala. At the feast. She was dancing and you watched her dance.'

Stevenson said nothing.

'Vaera was . . . hurt before she was killed,' Tootei said, as if looking for the right word.

'Yes, I know, Tootei. I was very, very sorry. I am very sorry.'

42

'She was fourteen years old. She was to be married. Her mother is sick in her mind with grief.'

Tootei said a few words in Samoan which Stevenson did not catch, and held something up to his face.

'This . . . This is yours?'

Stevenson looked down and saw that Tootei was holding a large-brimmed hat, crumpled in his huge brown fist. He stared at the hat and then at the man.

'Yesterday my son found this in a bush near the place where we discovered Vaera's body. My son says that your hat is like this one.'

'Yes, this looks like my hat. But mine is here, in the house.'

Stevenson looked at the hat again and then towards the line of pegs next to the entrance door. His hat was not there.

'Tootei, I understand how upset you must be and I too am very sorry, but surely your son doesn't think that I had anything to do with this. Maybe I dropped it the day you and I went up to the place, together.'

'You did not wear your hat that day. I remember. I thought you were more like us now, unafraid of the sun.'

'Tootei, please listen. I know this must be someone else's hat. Or perhaps someone took mine and lost it on the mountain. See here: if you wish, we'll speak to the chief justice once more. We will show him the hat and tell him where it was found. He will know what to do.'

Tootei threw the soiled hat on the floor.

'The chief is a white man,' he said.

'Only on his father's side. His mother was the daughter of Mataapaeia.'

'He is a white man, I tell you. He speaks like a white man. And you, Tusitala, are a white man. It will be useless to talk.' Then he walked out.

Stevenson was left standing, nauseated, in the empty hall.

*   *   *

He tried several times to tell Fanny about the hat but failed. During the last bout of his illness she had become sullen and distant. A few times during their marriage, he had seen her drift away into something like melancholy, and in that place she did not allow him to reach her. He felt unbearably sad. The house, which had given him at first so much joy as they set things up and made plans to enlarge rooms and extend the space, now seemed like a mausoleum, dank and dreary. What had once been new showed signs of decay, since in the tropical weather everything spoiled so quickly. Termites had burrowed into the furniture on the verandah: clouds of them had arrived one evening and, after dropping their wings, had scuttled through a hole in the wood, disappearing into tables and chairs, leaving a shower of silver scales on the floor behind them. A thin sheen of a grey moss-like substance covered the curtains they had ordered from France barely two years ago, and lacey cobwebs were strung across the corners of the window-frames, in spite of the daily cleaning by the servants. And his books, which he had brought over so carefully packed and labelled, were now speckled with green fungus and housed a tiny variety of beetles that laid their eggs deep between the signatures. Even the wax and varnish with which Fanny insisted his chair and desk be protected, seemed to have melted in the damp heat and stuck to his palms and wrists whenever he sat down to work.

He had not been able to get back to the book. He felt that he had abandoned his characters in mid-sentence, that he had lost them somewhere on the page, and that they were waiting in the dark for him to rescue them. But he felt useless, incapable of invention. He sat at his desk, thinking that perhaps, if he became physically active once again, the words would come. He fingered the ivory letter-opener, the rim of the silver inkpot, the stone tortoise carved in Chinese soapstone, the medal with the effigy of Bonnie Prince Charles. What could he invoke, he who had once said that God was merely another fiction? How this discovery had rattled his stern Presbyterian father, and with what despair the old man had written to his straying son a letter Stevenson had kept long after the rift was healed:

> *I have worked for you and gone out of my way for you – and the end of it is that I find you in opposition to the Lord Jesus Christ . . . I would ten times sooner see you lying in your grave than that you should be shaking the faith of other young men and bringing ruin on other houses as you have brought it upon this.*

It had taken many months before father and son were on speaking terms again, and though their very real love for one another was never quite in doubt, something changed forever after those words were written and read. As time went by and space and experience carried him far away from his father's house, a sense of belief in the unknowable, something like the intuition of faith crept back into his soul. But even now, so many years later, though he no longer denied the divinity, he still felt as someone left outside, on the threshold of a fine house, one long winter's night, waiting to be called in.

There was a knock on the door and one of the servants shyly told him that the chief justice wanted to see him.

The chief justice was a large man who always stood with his shoulders hunched, as if ashamed of his height. He smiled a lot, which put some people at ease and made others terribly uncomfortable, and he used this gift to great advantage. He liked Samoa's local celebrity, and the two men had enjoyed many

48

a long night of yarn-spinning and gossip. He sat in the chair facing Stevenson's and began to fan himself with a small paper fan.

'You're looking a fright, if you don't mind my saying so. This damp season, before the rains, you know is bad for the chest all round.'

'But good for growing things. Sosimo tells me that we're to have splendid crops next year.'

'Sosimo's right. Are you up to a conversation?'

'Friendly-like or professional?'

'Bit of both.'

'Go ahead. I imagine it's about Tootei's girl.'

'The family is broken over this. It was a terrible thing. Lovely wisp of a child, she was. Going to be married. Did Tootei tell you about the hat?'

'You think whoever did it dropped it there?'

'I think so, yes. There was a smear of

blood on the rim, as if he'd taken the hat off afterwards, holding it like this.'

The chief justice demonstrated with the fan.

'But why?'

'Why take off the hat? To wipe the sweat off his brow, maybe.'

'Yes, of course. Well, I don't think it's my hat, but I'm not certain.'

'Don't you have yours?'

'No, I can't find it. I must have lost it, but I can't remember when.'

'You had not been up the mountain recently?'

'Recently? No.'

The chief justice smiled broadly, drawing his neck in, like a turtle.

'I would never go up there, myself. Couldn't take the climb, you know.'

He fanned himself hard, as if the very thought of heat made him hotter. Then he asked:

'Have you seen any strangers around Vailima?'

'Strangers? No,' Stevenson answered too quickly.

'There've been rumours, you see. A certain missionary from your part of the world. Funny thing, these new arrivals. People here make up reputations for the newcomers. You understand what I mean. Someone new will arrive and immediately he'll be accused of every crime under the sun, and not a scrap of truth in any of it. Sometimes I will arrest one of them, you know, *pour encourager les autres.*'

'Oh, yes, I see. Mr Baker. Yes, I met him by chance on the beach. Harmless gentleman, I thought myself. Full of fire and brimstone, but I shouldn't imagine him capable of the slightest act of real violence. Too steeped in righteousness, if you know what I mean.'

'Quite so, quite so. Yes, all newcomers, especially if they are in the missionary trade, are preceded by wicked gossip. Sometimes it's the natives, but many times it's the rival missionaries themselves who compile these catalogues of atrocities for the benefit of their brethren. As far as I've heard, your Mr Baker has been accused of theft, rape, judicial murder, private poisoning, abortion, misappropriation of public moneys. Oddly enough not forgery, not arson.'

'Curious, isn't it, how thick the accusations fly in this South Sea world? I have no doubt my own character is something illustrious.'

'Only in the right sense, Mr Stevenson. Only in the right sense. And now, I think, I will trouble you no further.'

When the chief justice had left, Stevenson remained for a few minutes lost in thought. Then he picked up his pen, dipped it in the ink, and wrote:

We are evil, O God, and help us to see it and amend.

We are good and help us to be better. Look down upon Thy servants with a patient eye, Even as Thou sendest sun and rain; look down, Call upon the dry bones, quicken, enliven; Recreate in us the soul of service, the spirit of peace; Renew in us the sense of joy.

He wiped the pen and leaned back in his chair. This was not what he wanted to write, but the need for prayer had been stronger than his will to continue the story. He thought for a moment of Mr Baker, whom he had not seen (now he realised) in a very long time, and of whom he knew so little. He thought that Mr Baker would have approved.

It was almost December, the month of hot rain, and Stevenson had taken the cart into Apia to buy supplies with Sosimo. They had just finished with the order when he thought he saw the missionary enter the saloon at the corner of the market.

'That man,' he pointed quickly so that Sosimo might catch a glimpse of him. 'Do you know him?'

The overseer shook his head but the Chinese grocer answered spitting on the hardwood floor.

'I know that man. Only a week ago, he came in here and started to scream and shout about sin and perdition. Then he took one of my axes and began to break the liquor barrels. I called the market guards but it was too late. He had cracked six barrels and now no one will pay me for them.'

'What did the guards do?'

'He had left by the time they had arrived. And anyway, have you ever heard of a missionary being arrested in Samoa?'

'Why does he go to the saloon then?'

'Not to drink, that is for sure. He preaches there. He tries to make everyone's glass bitter by speaking of vinegar and gall.'

'Does he make converts?'

'No, but people run when they see him coming. The saloon keeper is not pleased.'

Leaving Sosimo to look after the loading of the goods, Stevenson crossed the road and entered the saloon. It took his eyes several minutes to get accustomed to the darkness. Then he saw Mr Baker in a far corner, talking to a native woman and holding her by the arm. When he noticed Stevenson, he let go and the woman escaped through the back door.

'I see that you have progressed from census-taking to Sunday preaching,' Stevenson said.

'The corruption here is so thick in the air that I find it hard to breathe. I show them what is to come, and they don't like the look of the everlasting fire.'

'I think you should finish your census and leave. The President is bound to hear of the complaints and then things may turn disagreeable for you.'

'It is not the President of this petty

municipality of Apia that I fear. Can't you smell the flames that are approaching? Can't you feel the heat and ashes in your nostrils? That is what I tell them but they are too far gone to heed to any warnings. That is what I explained to your chief justice. He came to see me. We talked.'

'Did he ask you about . . . about the events up on the mountain?'

'I told him that these things should not surprise him here. Everything is corrupt and loathsome. That girl was no loss. Did you think she was pretty?' Mr Baker's voice was slurred and tiny globs of white foam gathered at the corners of his mouth.

'I never met her.'

'Oh, I thought . . . Well, good riddance, in any case.'

'Don't say such things.'

'The day of reckoning is coming. Then we shall see what is lost and what is gained. Didn't your father once say those same words to you?'

The smoke, combined with a strong sweet smell like that of wilting jasmins which he only now seemed to notice, made him light-headed, and he found it difficult to focus on Mr Baker, who was swaying back and forth in his chair, pulling his glass dangerously close to the edge of the table. For a long moment, Stevenson was tempted to let the missionary sway further and further, and to hear the glass shatter on the hard floor. He forced himself to say, less as an offer than as an order:

'I shall walk you back to your lodgings.'

'You are right. I'll go. All this is indeed useless.'

They crossed the market and entered a maze of wet streets, which reeked of cabbage and fish. Down a small cul-de-sac they reached a wooden gate, a pathway of raised floodstones and then a creaking door that set a mob of invisible dogs barking. They climbed up two flights of rickety stairs and then stepped into a large unfurnished room, the entrance to which was protected by nothing more than a curtain of beads. Inside, a large woman was sitting on the floor, apparently feeding a group of children of various ages. Hearing them enter she turned and Stevenson saw the expression of sheer terror on her large face. Mr Baker did not even look in her direction but crossed the room and entered the next. Here too, Stevenson saw no furniture, except a makeshift bookshelf, with a few tattered volumes, a small, square table and a couple of bamboo chairs huddled in one corner, on the very edge of the rim of light shed by an oil lamp that hung from the ceiling.

'Bring us something to drink,' Mr Baker called out and then sat in one of the chairs, motioning his guest to the other. Stevenson heard scurrying and then a clatter of pans and dishes; finally a small black hand reached out from the darkness behind them and placed a carafe and two tumblers on the table.

Mr Baker poured out two drinks and pushed one of the tumblers towards Stevenson.

'Drink. If you are going to live in this hellish place, then you must make yourself strong in body as well as in spirit.'

'I thought you'd be a teetotaller,' said Stevenson.

'I am not, but they must be,' Mr Baker answered slowly. 'I can follow the road I know lies before me; for them, every drop is a further distraction. I would gladly let them burn in their own perdition, soak them in the alcohol which they seem so much to cherish, and set a match to the whole lot. I loathe this lost humanity.'

'Then what about me? Am I not a soul lost to drink?'

Mr Baker laughed. 'That is something you must decide on your own.'

'I will not deny myself a good glass and a dish. And I would not deny it to another fellow human. Love of life is a strong passion, and I have always followed its pull, even in trivial things such as food and drink.'

'Indeed?' Mr Baker said. 'Well, I deny that love is a strong passion. Fear is a strong passion; it is with fear that you must trifle, if you wish to taste the intensest joys of living.'

'I have my share of fear too, but I use it to love life all the more intensely.'

'Life that wastes your lungs down to a frayed gauze and makes you cough until your handkerchiefs are bloody?'

'The blood on my handkerchief is an accident, it doesn't colour my view of life. It has not hurt me, or changed me in any essential part.'

'So you say. If you could lead a healthy life at the cost of depriving all these wretches with not only liquor but of bread and water, you would do so. You would trade any man's soul for your own comfort.'

'You know that is not true.'

Mr Baker smiled. 'Fortunately, you do

not have the means to put such wager to the test.'

'But I wish I had, for your sake. I want to show you where I stand.'

There was a long silence, during which Stevenson watched Mr Baker's thin, unpleasant smile just within the ring of light on the other side of the table. He felt the need to break the silence.

'You are quite right. Our civilisation is a hollow fraud. All the fun of life is lost by it. All it gains is that a larger number of persons can continue to be contemporaneously unhappy on the surface of the globe. But there are so many moments of utter joy, glimpses of paradise, and for those I live. And yet I would not be the instrument of anybody's suffering for the sake of even one of those instants.'

Stevenson began to feel drowsy with the wine. He stared at the surrounding darkness and he thought he could make out, behind his host, thin dim contours of wavering light, as if damp or oily objects were shifting noise-lessly against the walls. Vaguely, as if just beyond the threshold of sound, he thought he heard laughter or singing, and also stifled sobbing, someone (he said to himself) who doesn't want anyone to know he is crying. The movement along the walls stopped and then started again, faintly obscene. Stevenson looked away.

Now his legs felt heavy, almost numb, but as he stretched them under the table, he had the impression of reaching into a vacuum, his feet stumbling into a hole in the wooden floor, so that he was forced to grip onto the arms of his bamboo chair to prevent himself from sliding or sinking away. He gasped and then felt embarrassed, and looked up to see whether Mr Baker had noticed, but the missionary had not changed his smile and, though he could not make out the man's eyes, he seemed to be looking back at Stevenson not with mockery but with pleasure.

Stevenson suddenly had the impression that many hours had passed since he had first entered the room with Mr Baker. Had his host been speaking just now? He couldn't tell. Next to the carafe, was once again full, sat a plate of small fried fish he had not noticed before, and their fixed black eyes appeared to him like the eyes of a single round creature, staring horribly at him from the middle of the table. What time was it? Somewhere, from a back room, came the ticking of a clock. Stevenson remembered the story of a monk who had been distracted from his copy-work by the song of a bird. He went into the garden to listen more closely, and when he returned, after what he thought were only a few minutes, he discovered that a century had gone by, that his fellow monks were dead and his ink had turned to dust. The song of the bird had given him a taste of Paradise, where an instant is as a hundred years of earthly time.

Was the same true of time in hell, Stevenson asked himself.

From inside the darkness, the small hand reached out to refill his glass. Stevenson watched the wine rise to the rim. He tried to stand up but the weight in his legs drew him back down. He managed to mouth the words to tell his host that he needed to get back, that Sosimo would be waiting for him. Then he passed out.

Vaguely he saw, as if in a half-dream, lying face upwards, the ceiling of the room as an immense circle in which the lamp stood round as an eye. He felt himself being carried, passing under other yellow ceilings and darkened rooms, and he heard moans and pleas and sobs, and hands trying to tear at his clothes and flesh. He felt hands rip at his breast, and a searing pain crossed his whole body. A horrible odour reached his nostrils, like that of decaying flesh, and then a burst of night air, hot but fresh. After that, he felt no more. Next day, Sosimo said he had found him fast asleep among the supplies in the back of the cart.

On Thursday the rains started, black sheets of water that hid everything from sight and drowned every other sound. Fanny had been very angry when he had told her what had happened, but in the morning rain, her mood seemed to change and by evening she was smiling. He had not been sick all day. In fact, he felt strong enough to accept the President's invitation to dinner that evening, in honour of some official or other. Normally, he disliked such gatherings, but tonight he wanted to celebrate. He knotted his tie in the mirror and watched his wife standing behind him, doing up her stays.

He cast back his mind to the afternoon when he had first met Fanny. It was the dusk of a summer's day, and a number of guests were sitting at table in the small hotel in Grez, near Fontainebleau. He had been walking in the woods with a knapsack on his back, feeling restored in the crisp French air, and, seeing dinner being served, had vaulted in through the open windows, much to the amusement of his friends. Among the guests were several he did not know, but the one who caught his attention was a dark-haired, full-mouthed American woman, accompanied by her seventeen-year-old daughter and her eight-year-old son. Fanny was twelve years his senior, a married woman who had left her awful husband in San Francisco and escaped to Europe. Her youngest son had caught influenza and died in Paris, and now here she was, in France with her two remaining children, to build up her life again. Stevenson said afterwards that he had never been so struck by the vitality and sheer force of a human face.

'You loved me because you thought I was the devil,' Fanny said to him soon after they were married. 'Everyone knows that beauty is of the fair blonde type. My gypsy dark skin told you to expect nothing from me but a wicked temper.'

A wicked temper indeed, but now she looked serene, as if the fire had turned to melancholy and the melancholy to calm which he hoped was a form of contentment. He took her hand, kissed it, and led her downstairs to the waiting cart.

The president's house in Apia declared itself to be the seat of government not because of its luxury or its superior style but merely because of its size. It was built on a slope overlooking the town, in exactly the same pattern as the other colonial houses of Apia, with a criss-crossed verandah, a white sloping roof like a truncated pyramid, which had to be repaired after each rainy season, and long shuttered windows which kept out the strongest rays of the sun but not the swarms of insects which descended at night, attracted

by the yellow petrol lamps. The Stevensons
were met by a native footman in uniform
who helped Fanny out and then nervously
took the reins of the mule.

While the president's wife led Fanny away to
meet 'the quite delightful Madame Verdein,'
(apparently the wife of a Belgian tradesman, a
devotee of Literature who had 'devoured every
line by Monsieur Stefansson' and was too shy
to encounter the Author himself but felt
herself worthy, however, of worshipping her
god's spouse), the president took Stevenson
into a corner and asked him please not to
make any reference to the 'German affair'
since several German businessmen were visiting Apia on official matters. Stevenson's
indignant letters to the papers concerning the
German bombing of a Samoan village had
provoked a diplomatic 'unpleasantness', and
after the recent tribal wars on the island, the
president was eager to keep things as quiet as
possible. He offered his guest a glass of wine.

Stevenson refused. 'Not that I wouldn't like one, but I've stopped all strong drink and smoke. Doctor's orders. And yet,' he laughed, 'I'm so made that I don't like to think of life without red wine on the table or without tobacco, with its lovely little coal of fire!'

'I wish there were more that would make those vows, I tell you. We've had the deuce of a spree of incidents all over the island, and much of it caused by drinking, I believe, beginning with that murderous rape up on the mountain. And now all sorts of beatings and destruction of property. The tribes are blaming one another, when they're not pointing fingers at the missionaries. Funk thinks there may be something in the liquor shipments. I heard they had a rash of violence like this in Tonga, a few years ago.'

'Indeed,' a voice behind them interrupted. The chief justice loomed over the two men, hunched and beaming. 'On one of the small offshore islets, a group of villagers thought the devil had possessed their friends, their parents, their brothers and sisters. So they hacked them to pieces, and burnt others on a pyre. Even small children. Ghastly business. It seems to come in different shapes wherever it arrives, this wave of madness. I'm not sure if it's what we're experiencing here, but apparently some of the missionaries are secretly consulting with the witch-doctors about joint exorcisms. Two godheads think better than one, it seems.' And the chief justice cackled uproariously.

'Is it us? Is it our intrusion that drives these people mad?' Stevenson asked. 'The petroglyphs up on the cliffs, you can barely make them out now, they are so dim and faded. The Samoans say those scrawlings are as old as the mountains themselves, written by the gods when the world was finished making. But now that we white folk have arrived, we've distracted the people from their worship of the gods, and so the gods have decided to erase their signature from their work. According to the gods, we, the intruders, are to blame.'

'Have you seen those petroglyphs yourself?' asked the chief justice.

'Yes, what is left of them,' Stevenson answered.

'That's not when you lost your hat, was it?'

'Your hat?' asked the president.

Stevenson answered: 'The chief justice believes that the hat found next to the girl's body was mine.'

'No, no, of course not! Please don't misinterpret me,' the chief justice pleaded.

'I lose a hat every week in this place,' the president smiled. 'You take it off to wipe your forehead, put it down and it's gone.'

From the corner of his eye, Stevenson saw Fanny approaching, led by a vast woman in a lace-edged mumu.

'Robert, Madame Verdein wants to meet you but she's too timid.'

Stevenson smiled.

'She seems to think she saw you, earlier this evening, in the market. I told her it must have been your *fetch*.'

'*Fetch*?' asked the plump lady.

'A ghost, Madame. The disembodied image of a living person. It is supposed to foretell death,' Stevenson explained.

'How horrible,' said the lady with a shiver.

'Robert, that's not always the case, is it? I thought it was more like someone's shadow, a shadow with a life of its own.'

'We call those *adaro* here,' said the chief justice. 'But they don't look like the body they inhabit. They look like birds.'

'Bird, shadow or *fetch*, I was not at the market today, Madame Verdein.'

Suddenly there was a commotion in the main hall. The president excused himself. The chief justice followed him. The guests were flocking out onto the verandah.

'Fire!' someone cried.

Stevenson, Fanny and Madame Verdein

peered over the eager heads, down on the town below. Flames were rising from somewhere in the town centre and black smoke was billowing up against the clear night sky.

'What is it?' Stevenson asked.

'The saloon, they say. Blaze is up,' one of the guests answered.

The chief justice put a hand on Stevenson's shoulder.

'I must be off.'

'Let me go with you,' Stevenson said.

Fanny objected. 'Robert, the smoke.'

'I'll be all right. I won't be long.'

They climbed into the chief justice's cart and drove down through the clear-cut path. Once they reached the market area it was impossible to break through the crowd. At last they got out and ran, Stevenson surprised at the chief justice's swiftness and at the docility of his own lungs. The heat reached them before they were able to break through the throng of onlookers. The chief justice saw one of his assistants somewhere ahead of the crowd and shouted out a question in Samoan. He translated the answer for Stevenson:

'The doors are locked and people are trapped inside. They've gone to get axes.'

Now, among the shouts of the crowd and the crackling of the fire, Stevenson heard the screams, shrill and long, like those of frightened animals.

'How many?'

'No one knows. But at this time, the saloon is pretty full. Plus the women, of course.'

The chief justice pushed his way through, and Stevenson followed. The smoke was thick, and as they moved closer, Stevenson felt himself starting to choke but could not pull himself away. Several men had begun hacking at the doors of the saloon with their axes. Thick dark arms flailed wildly through the small barred windows. Pails of water, passed along a human chain, were flung uselessly on the flames. The heat was powerful.

At last the doors were broken. There was a burst of flames as the night air fed the fire, and then, for a long moment, a hideous and eerie silence. Wrapping themselves in pieces of wet cloth, five or six men braved the furnace. A moment later, Stevenson saw them carry out a vaguely human form, black as coal. A loud wail rose from the crowd. Two, three more bodies were hauled out. Then, with a sickening snap, the beams of the roof caved in, trapping one of the rescuers. The chief justice was bellowing out orders, seemingly to no one in particular. A child began to cry.

One of the women in the crowd pointed a finger and shouted. Several heads turned to look. Suddenly, Stevenson realised that they were staring at him. The woman continued to shout. Other voices joined in. The crowd moved towards him. The chief justice grabbed him by the arm.

'Come away.'

'What is it? What are they saying?'

'Come away. She says she saw you here, carrying an oil lamp. She's accusing you of stoking the fire?'

'Me? But that is absurd!' Stevenson started to protest but the chief justice was a strong man. As they turned the corner, a volley of small stones flew past their backs. Stevenson felt a blow on his left shoulder.

'Crowds need to find a victim,' the chief justice said when they had returned to the cart by drawing a wide loop through the back streets.

'But can't you tell them that I was with you, that you saw me at the President's house?'

'They wouldn't listen. They tell their own stories. And they believe them, too.'

A week later Sosimo drove his master into town once again. But this time, when they reached the general store, they found the doors shut and the blinds down. The Chinese

owner, who always prided himself in attend-
ing the local celebrity, was sitting on a low
bamboo rocking-chair, still as a stone.

'Will you not open?' Stevenson said after
greeting him. 'We need a few things.'

The man didn't answer. Instead, he slowly
lifted himself out of the chair and started to
waddle towards the back of the building.

Stevenson ran after him, but the old man
shook him off and disappeared through a side
door. Stevenson stood still for a few minutes,
uncertain of what to do, and then turned
towards Sosimo who had been watching the
proceedings from the cart.

'Sosimo, do you know what is happening?'

Sosimo shrugged his shoulders. A small
boy, probably the old man's grandson, peeked
through a grimy window and then disappeared, pulled back by a large hand. A few
seconds later he reappeared from behind the
house, staring at the thin white man who was
standing on the stairs of his family shop.

'Why are you closed?' Stevenson asked him.

'Not closed,' the boy answered.

'Not closed? Then why is the door locked? Why won't your grandfather let us in? Go tell him we need to buy things.'

'Others can buy,' the boy said. 'But not you.'

'Not me? But why?' Stevenson felt suddenly foolish, demanding explanations from a six-year-old.

'Because you are bad, grandfather says,' the boy answered and ran back from where he had come.

'Bad? Bad?' Stevenson repeated out loud to himself. Then he turned again to Sosimo.

'Sosimo, what does all this mean?'

'It doesn't matter. We will have to shop at the other store, the one across the bridge,' said the practical man. 'They will be open.'

The other store, a ramshackle construction which held barely more than a few sacks of flour, cones of sugar, candles, rum and tobacco, was run by a drunken old Frenchman who had come to Samoa so long ago that no one could remember when. His stock was always limited because he hardly ever paid his suppliers, and the women didn't like to go there because he would ogle them with red-rimmed eyes and say nothing. Now he sat on a three-legged stool and swatted at the flies. Sosimo climbed down from the cart and, with a look of distaste, started selecting a few things from under the counter. Suddenly, from the corner of his eye, Stevenson saw another figure sitting in the speckled shade of a breadfruit tree. He recognized him at once but the seated man gave no sign of welcome.

'Mr Baker?' Stevenson asked.

'I suppose I should thank you.'

'Thank me, Mr Baker? What for?'

'For your hand in cleaning this damned island. For putting a stop to their filthy business in the town.'

'What are you talking about?'

'We spoke of fire that night, in my rooms. Of the cleansing fire that is a foretaste of the fires to come. I knew you would understand. You hate them too.'

'Hate them? What do you mean?'

'You ask yourself why you must suffer while they laugh and drink and fornicate. You ask why your lungs must rot when they, who can barely think and drag their miserable lives further and further away from God, can breathe easily. You hate them too because you look on that sound flesh and you know that it is there to tempt you into wanting it. And you know that this place cannot be purified without destruction.'

'You are mad.'

'Not at all. Your will is stronger than you suppose, and when challenged it can work wonders. You were seen in the saloon before the fire broke out.'

'That is absurd, I was at the President's house.'

Mr Baker let out a short, clipped laugh and said again: 'Yes, I know. But nevertheless, thank you. Your help was much appreciated.'

Without another word, Stevenson hurried back to the cart, streams of sweat running down his face and neck, and waited for Sosimo to finish loading. Later, in the small breeze which rose as they drove away, he felt no relief whatsoever.

Fanny was still asleep when Stevenson woke up the next morning. He dressed and went outside just as the sun was rising, the first hot rays hitting the roots and lowest branches of the bushes around the verandah, leaving the rest hidden in darkness. The air was gold with dust.

He heard a rustle among the leaves and then noticed Tootei's round figure emerge and stand stock-still on the path, facing him. Stevenson called out 'good morning', but Tootei didn't answer, and for a while the two men stood looking at each other in the growing light. Then Tootei spoke:

'Tusitala, I know the story.'

'The story, Tootei?'

'The story of what happened on the mountain, and the story of what happened in the saloon. It is all one story, and Tusitala knows it too.'

'I don't know it, Tootei. Tell it to me.'

'The story begins like one of the stories you tell us, Tusitala. It begins with the arrival of a man on an island. The man brings many things from his home – his bed, his table, his books, his wife – and begins to build himself a house. But the things he has brought with him are not good for the island, or maybe the island does not like those things. And so his bed grows damp and unhealthy, and his table will not serve up wholesome food, and his books refuse to speak to him, and his wife grows distant and unattractive. And so the man begins to desire other things that are not his but the island's. He does not say so, but at night he dreams of all that is beyond his lawful grasp: a place to sleep in comfort, a body that is not weak, a wife that will give and receive pleasure. All these things are on the island and are his in his dreams, but he dares not take them in the morning. And the longing makes him sick. Then, one day, the longing grows so strong that it leaves the man and sets off on its own, like a hunter, without waiting for the morning. All night it hunts and then, after it has taken its prey, it sleeps, and the man knows nothing of it. One day the man sees what his longing has done, the foul deeds and the trail of blood, but he refuses to believe it. "I am the master of my desire," the man says, and closes his eyes. So the deeds continue and the man still refuses to see, until one morning he finds that he is no longer dreaming his longing, but his longing is dreaming him. He is in a dream on the top of a mountain and in the dream he sees

a young girl whom his longing can not forget. And he takes the young girl, and forces her for his pleasure. And when she screams out, he kills her.

And then he awakes, and his longing says to him, "You have done well, now think no more about it." And night after night the man's longing fetches him out and takes him to strange places and asks him to do things that he forgets in the morning, until the dreams themselves become unbearable and the man no longer wishes to sleep. That is the story, Tusitala. You killed my daughter, and you set fire to the saloon where my son burned to death, and now I will put an end to your story-telling. I will kill you.'

Stevenson saw the flash of the blade as it caught the light of the sun, and, without thinking, he fell to one side as Tootei lunged towards him. For a moment, Tootei's round face pressed against his, as if he were about to kiss him, and then, as Stevenson tried to lift one knee against his assailant, he heard a sound like a long whisper, and a groan, and Tootei's full weight collapsed over him. The large black limbs shook and then went limp, and Stevenson found it difficult to breathe. Slowly, with a great effort, he pulled himself from under Tootei's body. Then he lay in the dust, wheezing, next to the dead man whose eyes were still open. A pool of Tootei's blood began to spread towards him, and as Stevenson tried to lift himself, it seemed to grow brighter and brighter. He felt drained of all strength. He did not move until the wetness reached his hand.

This time, it was a whole week before he fully regained consciousness. Fanny told him afterwards that Sosimo had found him outside and carried him to his bed. Dr Funk had been called in, and the chief justice too, and while the former had ministered to the patient, the latter had carted off the body of Tootei to be buried by his family. It had not seemed necessary to have an inquest, since what had happened was obvious to anyone. Tootei had tried to attack Stevenson in a fit of insanity brought on by grief after the loss of his two children, and had fallen on his own knife. 'The least publicity', the chief justice had said, 'the better.' Fanny had thanked him with all her heart.

When Stevenson woke, with a salty taste in his mouth and a deep pain in his left side, he couldn't tell whether it was day or night. A dim light filtered through the shutters. First he thought it was the moon; then he heard voices and knew it must be daytime.

Fanny entered carrying a basin and a cloth, and sat down by his side to wash his face. There were a few specks of coughed-up blood caught in the stubble on his chin. He looked at her gratefully, and she started.

'You're awake. You've been asleep for so long.'

'Did I say anything?'

'You were coughing terribly, and you lost much blood. I wouldn't let you speak; trying to speak made you cough even harder. Once or twice you said my name. And Tootei's. You called out to him.'

'Nothing else?'

'At one point I thought you might be praying, you were mumbling words as if reciting something. But I could not make out what it was. My poor dear, I was so afraid for you.' And she put down the basin and held both his hands.

He slept a while, but a different sort of sleep, far more quiet and refreshing than any he had enjoyed in a long time. He opened his eyes and now he knew it was night-time. The air was cool. Suddenly he saw a figure standing at the foot of the bed. He tried to lift himself when he realised who it was, but fell back against the pillows.

'What are you doing here?'

'It is nothing but a friendly visit,' said Mr Baker. 'I thought I'd come and see for myself this joy of life that you are always on about. But what I see are the rings under the eyes and the hair wet with sweat, and the rasping breath and the blood-stained handkerchiefs. And I can't help but imagine the long, drawn-out nights when the wind isn't stirring and all you can hear is the drilling buzz of the mosquitoes. If I were you, my friend, I don't know that I'd be able to carry on. What for? These are the wages of sin, and they are paid beyond the pale of redemption. If I were you, I would put an end to it all, curse God and die.'

Stevenson lay very still, knowing that the slightest movement would re-start the flow. He spoke with deliberate slowness.

'I know my time will come soon enough, but I will not dwell on it. What is the purpose? We might as well dwell on the work of our teeth or on the mechanics of our walk. It is there, it will always be there, and I don't intend to spend my glorious hours looking over my shoulder to see death's icy face.'

'I suppose you know what you have done.'

'Done?'

'Your undertakings. Your hand as the instrument of God. A soldier in His army. I much admire you.'

'You don't know what you're saying.'

'But I do, and you know that I do. Through the flesh to punish the flesh, and through blood to punish blood. There was no sin in your killings. The girl, her brother, the old man, they were all enemies of the True Cause. What does it matter if it was to satisfy your own longing?'

'I killed no one. I won't let you say so.'

'Whether it was your hand or mine, or fate if you like, what does it matter? You wanted her, your longing had to have her, and so I took her for you. You loathed the blaspheming, drunken crowds, because they were full of life while yours is ebbing away, and so I did away with them to please you. The deed is done, and the longing was yours. We are all characters in the same story, as you yourself said sometime, and our parts are interchangeable, even that of the story-teller. And as the story-teller, you know that what desire conjures up in your dreams becomes part of the dust we touch and the air we see. Why refuse to believe it? Why not accept it? Don't you remember *Religio Medici*, that passage you are so fond of?'

Mr Baker took a book from Stevenson's bookshelf as surely as if this were his own room. He opened it to a page marked with a yellow slip of paper. He read:

To see our selves again, we need not look for Plato's year: every man is not only himself: there hath been many Diogenes and as many Timons, though but few of that name: men are liv'd over again, the world is now as it was in Ages past; there was none then, but there hath been some one since that parallels him, and is, as it were, his revived self.

Stevenson tried again to lift himself from his pillows but the effort was too great. He fell back, closing his eyes, and Mr Baker, quietly, put the book by the side of his bed.

'Now that you've understood this, I need not come again. Farewell, my brother.'

When Stevenson opened his eyes again, Mr Baker was gone.

Stevenson recovered enough to sit up in bed and, after a few days, to stroll through the house and the garden. He walked along the path which, in spite of Sosimo's efforts, seemed never to be clear of vegetation: the roots and trailers that grew back almost immediately after they were cut, the fallen fruit that spilled the shiny seeds from the flesh open as if wounded, the large leaves that strings of ants ferried from wilderness to wilderness. He crossed the breadfruit grove and stepped out into the sun. Here he stopped and stared, with a curious sense of relief, at what he called his island. A horse stood alone in the long grass swatting flies with its tail, and beyond it the trail wound itself red as a scar up the mountain-side. 'Death to the optic nerve,' Stevenson repeated to himself, but it was useless because the landscape unfurled itself like a scroll and he felt obliged to read the writing on it, the colours, the shapes, the patterns and sequences, which he translated into words, almost unconsciously, like a man unable to stop speaking to himself.

He tried not to think of what had happened. Here, in the green heat, that which was forbidden was not mentioned. Evil was tabu, unuttered, it was not given existence in words. On the stones of Edinburgh was written, in the Gothic script that had so delighted Sir Walter Scott in his youth, the Old Testament warning, Thou Shalt Not, so that during Stevenson's wanderings through the city his eye would always land, unbidden, on the outlawed temptations, the sins spelled out for all to know, offered as in a dark mirror even to those who had not yet conceived them, like an inverted pleasure.

A week or so later, he was back at his work-table, writing. He felt curiously excited, and yet uneasy, as if he had woken from an unpleasant dream that he could not remember. Fanny tried to make him stay in bed at least part of the day, but to no avail. He told her that the new story was coming together too quickly, and he had to catch up with it, or it would escape him forever.

He worked all morning, and in the afternoon he brought his morning's work to Fanny and asked her whether he had not done well. The voice of Mr Baker, the gestures of the poor dead girl, the horrible lodgings with its strange inhabitants, even his own revolting dreams were transformed into the story, and the South Seas stood now frozen into a northern landscape, in which the flame-trees were churches and the brooks busy streets. In her glow of admiring assent he found his confirmation and his reward.

Now the mail fell to be answered; not the business correspondence – for this was left till later – but replies to the long, kindly letters of distant friends, received but two days since, and still bright in memory. He set himself to work and the hours slid gently by.

At sunset he came downstairs, rallied Fanny about the sudden grey mood she said she could not shake off, talked of a lecturing tour to America that he was eager to make 'as I'm feeling so well', and played a game of cards with her to drive away her melancholy.

He said he was hungry, begged her assistance to make a salad for the evening meal and, to enhance the little feast, he brought up a bottle of old Burgundy from the cellar. He was helping Fanny on the verandah and gaily talking, when suddenly he put both hands to his head and cried out:

'What is it?'

He fell on his knees beside her. He shouted out:

'Has my face changed?'

Fanny screamed for help and Sosimo came running in. Between the two, they helped him into the great hall and laid him back in the armchair that had once been his grandfather's. Fanny bent down to kiss him. He had already lost consciousness.

Dr Funk was called in, but all he did was look at him and shake his head. Stevenson had passed on to where nothing and no one could further help or reach him.

Note on the Text

Certain names (including that of Mr Baker from Tonga), certain expressions and descriptions have been taken from *The Letters of Robert Louis Stevenson to His Family and Friends*, selected and edited, with notes and introduction by Sydney Colvin, 2 vols., Charles Scribner's Sons, New York, 1899.

Note on the Woodcuts

The woodcuts which illustrate this little text were made by Stevenson himself while he was convalescing in the sanatorium town of Davos, Switzerland, in 1881, accompanied by Fanny and her twelve-year-old son. The young Lloyd Osbourne occupied his days with a toy theatre, an army of tin soldiers and a small printing press – all gifts from his literary step-father. One day, "with an affected humility that was most embarrassing," Stevenson arrived carrying a manuscript entitled *Not I, and Other Poems*, which he submitted to the young printer. It was immediately accepted and the first edition of fifty copies sold out in no time. Stevenson's next offering was a collection of short ditties, *Moral Emblems*, which he decided to illustrate with his own woodcuts. A consumptive Swiss who made his living carving bears agreed to reproduce them for the press. *Moral Emblems* was published in a print-run of ninety copies, at the reasonable price of sixpence each.